THE BEST ME I CAN BE™

I Will Keep Trying!

by David Parker
Illustrated by Marcy Dunn Ramsey

SCHOLASTIC INC.
New York Toronto London Auckland Sydney
Mexico City New Delhi Hong Kong Buenos Aires

Each day is another opportunity to make it better.
— D.P.

To my dear brother Marty, one of the most "trying" people I know...
— M.D.R.

ISBN 0-439-73588-2

Text copyright © 2005 by David Parker
Illustrations copyright © 2005 by Marcy Dunn Ramsey
All rights reserved. Published by Scholastic Inc.
SCHOLASTIC, THE BEST ME I CAN BE™ Readers, and associated logos are trademarks and/or
registered trademarks of Scholastic Inc.

12 11 10 9 8 7 6 5 4 3 2 1   5 6 7 8 9 10/0

Printed in the U.S.A.
First printing, January 2005

Sometimes it may be hard to read
all the words in a book.

Sometimes it may be hard to write your name and stay in the lines.

Sometimes it may be hard to tell
what time it is.

Try it once. Try it twice. Try it several more times.
Maybe you will do it this time!

Sometimes it may be hard to know
the right answer in math.

Sometimes it may be hard to make a new friend.

Sometimes it may be hard to order food in a restaurant.

Try it once. Try it twice. Try it several more times.
Maybe you will do it this time!

Sometimes it may be hard to know
the right bus to get on.

Sometimes it may be hard to ride
a bike with two wheels.

Sometimes it may be hard to remember your phone number and address.

Sometimes it may be hard to set
the table yourself.

Try it once. Try it twice. Try it several more times. Maybe you will do it this time!

What is something you keep trying to do?